Copyright Emma E. Murray, 2024

Published by Archive of the Odd

Formatting and cover design by Cormack Baldwin

Content warnings can be found at the back of this book.

This is a work of fiction. All characters and events are fictitious. Any resemblance to actual persons, living or dead, or events, present or historical, are coincidental.

All rights reserved. Reproduction and transmission of this production by any means, including mechanical, audio, or electronic, without prior permission of the publisher and copyright holder is prohibited.

ISBN 979-8-9884827-2-7

BLOOD, SWEAT, & TEARS

EXTREME PERFORMANCE ART

Welcome to The Museum of Modern Art's audio tour, specifically designed for the visually impaired, of our latest exhibit, Blood, Sweat, and Tears: Extreme Performance Art. Please proceed along the textured path and when the device detects a piece, an in-depth description will commence. When a piece has incorporated a tactile element, that will be indicated as well as instructions for interaction. We hope you enjoy your visit.

To your right, you are approaching the work of Juniper Fleiss. To hear more, please step onto the metal plate.

Artist plaque: Juniper Fleiss's body of work is well known and celebrated, though her final piece has caused considerable controversy and censorship. Here, we have curated photographs, interviews, and explanations of her extreme performance pieces and their impact on the art world.

The first piece in our collection is "Tooth Fairy," 2014. The jar containing the teeth from the performance are available on the ledge to your left to be handled with care. Please do not shake or flip the jar and ensure it is returned safely to its display when finished.

Excerpt from Interview with Fleiss regarding *Tooth Fairy*, June 4, 2014, New York Art Magazine

Reporter: Your latest performance has caused quite a stir with some saying it shouldn't be considered art. Can you tell us a little about the piece and what you meant viewers to take away from the spectacle?

Fleiss: You should know that I don't tell my viewers what meaning to take from my art. They will find the meaning that they want to find, or perhaps, need to find. About the performance, it was quite painful. Both the ingestion and subsequent passing. Delilah's milk teeth were easier to swallow, though a few of the molars stuck in my throat. My own teeth, however, were especially jagged and the raw pain from their removal certainly didn't help, but it was all part of the performance.

Reporter: Was the performance something you'd been planning for a long time or was it one of your more spontaneous bursts of inspiration?

Fleiss: I'd been keeping Delilah's teeth in a small box, lined with satin, knowing they would factor somehow into a piece eventually. I'd originally thought they'd be fastened to a painting or perhaps incorporated into a sculpture, but the muse found me that summer morning and I knew I had to go to the square straight away and commence the public performance instead. I wasn't completely sure what I would do until I was there, sitting in the gray light of the overcast morning, people bustling around on their bicycles and on foot, no one caring about the strange woman sitting cross-legged in the center of it all with a box in one hand and her own teeth in the other, the hot strings of bloody saliva still streaming down her chin and sullying her blouse, and then I knew. And as soon as I'd started the performance, the bustle stopped, everyone frozen in time, frozen in terror, and watching. Taking what they needed from my pain, whether it be their own empathetic pain or pleasure, and I was sure it was a work worthwhile.

Reporter: There are some rumors about how your own teeth were collected. Of course, there's the possibility you met with an unfortunate accident or even took some tool to your own mouth, but since you say you weren't sure of the performance until it began, I can't help but think of the theory that your partner, Claude Moulin, might've struck you and knocked the teeth out, perhaps bringing with it the inspiration for the piece?

Fleiss: I don't comment on rumors.

Reporter: But Claude has a documented history of domestic violence, with police records indicating you yourself have called the authorities on him for assault multiple times. If you could clear up the rumors, then the debate on whether the piece is a commentary on abuse could be resolved.

Fleiss: I refuse to comment on those allegations. As I said, the art speaks for itself, and those who view or study it can find the truth they wish to find.

Reporter: Understood. Now, the consumption was public, but you were prevented from publicly performing the excretion due to decency laws. However, the final product is now viewable in the museum of modern art. Is there anything else you'd like to share about the performance?

Fleiss: I was quite disappointed that the entire act was not viewed by the public, as I consider the excretion just as important for the performance as the swallowing, and it was indeed twice as painful, but the museum did graciously allow me to perform the cleaning and placement of the teeth in their jar, though behind a clear barrier to limit the smell for any viewers. Around forty people attended the meticulous cleaning of the teeth and heard each one clink into the jar, which is now available to be held and gently shaken for anyone who wants to ponder the meaning of the piece.

Reporter: Are there any hints or ideas you'd like to share with your fans for upcoming performances?

Fleiss: Only to keep your eyes open, as I could be anywhere at any time, and that I will continue to push the boundaries of what is considered art, as well as what it is to be human.

The jar you are invited to hold and explore through sound and touch is clear with no label and contains the twenty small milk teeth of Fleiss's daughter Delilah

Moulin as well as Fleiss's own top four incisors. All the teeth have been scrubbed but still retain dark traces of blood and excrement in their naturally occurring grooves. Notice the subtle pleasant sound when lightly shaken and take your time to imagine the meaning behind this excruciating and personal piece.

The next piece in this collection is formally untitled, but commonly referred to as "Balcony Endurance Piece." An embossed version of one of the photographs is included to deepen the experience for our visually impaired visitors. Feel free to explore the textured version while the performance is described, and the recovered chat logs are read.

Untitled Endurance Piece, 2016, photograph description

Fleiss stands on a third-floor balcony of a hotel, arms stretched out to form a cross. She wears only a thin nightgown, her petite nude frame clearly visible through the near-transparent fabric, and her long dark hair is unfastened, whipped by the intense winds of the day. One of her eyes is visibly darkened, later confirmed to be a "black eye" bruise. The sky is overcast, and records show the temperature at the time of the performance was just below freezing. Below, onlookers gather and watch, some pointing, their mouths open with shouts, and some standing silently. The crowd did not gather until her performance had reached the two-hour mark and someone had noted her distinct appearance and realized the act for what it was. She continued the performance for a further five hours after this photograph was taken before slowly lowering her arms, concluding the piece at just over seven hours, and retiring back through the doors of the balcony to her room.

Untitled Endurance Piece, 2016, recovered chat log, pertinent transcript excerpts from before and after

The following chat logs are between Fleiss and longtime friend and paramour, Sheila Williams. They were released years after the performance by the artist to give greater clarity to the meaning of the performance and as part of a custody dispute with open records.

TheArtisteYouHate: He did it again.

Sheba6779: No
Sheba6779: You're kidding

TheArtisteYouHate: Dead serious.

Sheba6779: You've gotta get outta there
Sheba6779: Take Delilah and come stay with me. I'll be good. She doesn't have to know.

TheArtisteYouHate: Not now. He'll just use it against me.
TheArtisteYouHate: It's gonna be a black eye. Fuck. And a dark one. Hard to hide.

Sheba6779: Fuck

TheArtisteYouHate: Tore out some of my hair too. There's a bald spot, that's how much he yanked out. It burns still, but not really bleeding.

Sheba6779: Cuz of me?

TheArtisteYouHate: Nothing bad is ever because of you, sweetheart.

Sheba6779: What are you going to do if you won't come here?

TheArtisteYouHate: The cold calls. Maybe a performance is overdue.

Continued excerpt from after the performance, more than 8 hours later

TheArtisteYouHate: I'm back. Thanks for making sure to get eyes on it. My arms hurt so bad, but it was worth it. Took a shower. I feel much better.

Sheba6779: It was spectacular as always. The posture, the bruising prominent, the nightgown, even when you soiled yourself at the six-hour mark, it all worked together beautifully. There's no way there will be any confusion about the symbolism behind this one, and I heard from a little bird that there will be an article about it up as soon as tomorrow.

TheArtisteYouHate: Thank you, darling. The crowd was more impressive than I'd expected.

Sheba6779: Looked to be around three hundred to me
Sheba6779: So what did he say?

TheArtisteYouHate: He left.
TheArtisteYouHate: Not answering my calls or texts.
TheArtisteYouHate: He took Delilah.
TheArtisteYouHate: I don't worry he'll hurt her, only keep her away from me.

Sheba6779: Are you sure? Should you call the police?

TheArtisteYouHate: No.

TheArtisteYouHate: He'll do what hurts me the most and hide her, but I'll find her.

Sheba6779: Come here and I'll comfort you

TheArtisteYouHate: Can't. I need to find Delilah first.
TheArtisteYouHate: Later.

Sheba6779: okay sweetheart. You were incredible. Rest and revel in the statement you made for women like you all over the world, hidden in the shadows and behind closed curtains

TheArtisteYouHate: You always know the right thing to say. Come to the hotel. Room 335. He won't be back tonight anyway.

The next piece is one of Fleiss's most well-known, titled "Maiden, Mother, Crone," and one that ended in disaster for her personal life despite the performance's great success and acclaim. A video of the performance will play with narrated description provided between speaking segments. Following this, the artist's response to the various outrage and accolades, posted on her website, will be read aloud.

Maiden, Mother, Crone, 2017, clips from video recording of performance

Clip 1:
(Heavy curtains are undraped to reveal three pedestals with a person standing on each and a projection behind them of real footage of a woman giving birth.)

9

Fleiss: Society tells us there are only three stages of a woman's life, maiden, mother, crone. Each worth less than the last. Look upon us. We are here for your jeers, leers, and judgment. Take us apart and toss us aside. What makes a woman's value so different from that of a man? What makes you so repulsed by age and so enticed by youth? Come. We are here for the taking. Do as you wish. Mold us to your liking until we are acceptable again.

(On the first pedestal, approximately three feet off the ground, a glass box encases Fleiss's young daughter Delilah, aged eleven. She is dressed in a yellow summer dress and her dark hair tied up with a matching bow. An assortment of markers is scattered around the base of her stand. The next pedestal has the artist on it, in the open and lower than the first by a foot, completely nude with arms outstretched and eyes closed as soon as she finished her speech. The third pedestal is mere inches off the ground and an elderly woman stands on it, also fully nude and with closed eyes. A variety of instruments are scattered on the floor between these last two pedestals, including markers, needles and thread, a hatchet, scissors, scarves, various kinds of makeup like lipstick and blush, clothespins, flowers, and ribbons)

Sounds of crowd quietly mumbling and shuffling around the exhibit. Marker cap clicks and screeches as two observers draw hearts, happy faces, and sign their names on the glass encasing Delilah.

Man 1: I'm gonna give her a haircut.
Woman 1: No, don't.

Woman 2: It's okay. That's the sort of thing she wants us to do, don't you see? Fashion her to our liking.
Soft laughter from the crowd and squealing shoes against flooring.
Snip of scissors through hair.

(Man 1 has climbed onto the platform and is cutting Fleiss's hair into a blunt bob. She remains motionless with closed eyes. The hair falls around her feet and off the platform onto the floor below)

Clip 2, four hours into performance:

(The elderly woman has been smeared with makeup, the skin on her face pulled taut with clothes pins, and the scarves wrapped around her body to hide her nudity. Fleiss has had her hair shorn, vulgar words written across her body, and a threaded needle pushed through her lip but then the assaulter's plan aborted seemingly by the large quantity of blood it produced. The daughter's glass has become riddled with vulgar phrases and drawings, some scratched out or scribbled over but many still visible)

Man 2 (pounding on glass case around Delilah): Open up and let me draw on you like the others.
Guard: Come with me. I've told you twice already, that's beyond the scope of the piece—
Man 2: Get off me. It's just part of the art. I just wanna hold her…

(The man reaches into his pants and begins to masturbate)

Guard: That's it. You're gone.

Man 2: Try your best.

(The man grabs the hatchet, threatens the guard who leaves to get backup. The man then flings the hatchet at the glass case around Delilah, which shatters.)

Mixed voices: screaming, crying, unintelligible yelling.

(The man attempts to pull the girl off the pedestal while she screams before the guard and two policemen return and the clip ends)

Delilah was quickly recovered unscathed, though thoroughly shaken, and the performance immediately halted. After a deluge of commentary across all platforms, Fleiss posted the following statement to her website in response to the outrage.

Response to *Maiden, Mother, Crone*, August 8, 2017

To the public, the viewers, those who got it and those who didn't,

I hear you all.

It was irresponsible of me to have my daughter as part of the performance, even with the safety measures put in place. Obviously, they were not enough, and despite the piece reflecting exactly the dark, twisted side of humanity it had intended to unveil, it was not worth the price to my daughter's mental health. She is in therapy working through the incident, and the many angry parents who have sent hate mail and threats, you will be happy to know that my ex-partner has been granted temporary full custody of her while we work things out.

I love my daughter, and I disagree with the courts and my critics, but it is what it is for now. I only share this intimate part of my life with you all because I know it will calm many hearts and hopefully lessen the constant harassment I've been faced with.

For those who understood the art for what it was, and appreciated what it showed the world, thank you for standing with me. I appreciate every one of you who has reached out in even the smallest ways. It is a dark time in my life and the outpouring of love and understanding has meant so much.

My next performance piece has been postponed and changed direction after the recent events, but it will happen. Keep your eyes peeled and know we are none of us ever truly safe, even in our most private moments.

Your object,
Juniper Fleiss

Fleiss's next performance was six months later, the infamous piece "Streaming," where she live-streamed every second of her life for two weeks via a camera she wore as a pendant around her neck, capturing many beautiful private moments but also showing her viewers how bad the harassment from her detractors had become. At various points, she was yelled at, had a smoothie tossed on her car windshield, and ultimately, was sexually assaulted in the elevator of her own apartment building. The assailant was quickly arrested, but the footage went viral on various social media and brought new eyes onto Fleiss's work.

Excerpt from Interview with Fleiss regarding *Streaming*, March 16, 2018, New York Art Magazine

Reporter: Thank you for this rare interview. We know you've been very guarded and private since the conclusion of "Streaming" a little over a month ago, and for good reason.

Fleiss: Let's be clear, I will not be discussing the assault. It happened, it was recorded, it was part of the work, for better or worse, but I won't say any more about it beyond that the man who attacked me is currently in prison awaiting trial.

Reporter: Of course. We wouldn't want to exploit your trauma.

Fleiss: Oh, you wouldn't?

Reporter: No, never. We're not that kind of publication.

Fleiss: All media is "that kind" of media. That's what the piece was all about, don't you see? We are all voyeurs and I accept that. I just don't want to talk about the incident, but there's no denying the human instinct to pry, to judge, to be scandalized.

I've been asked if I'll scrub the footage from the internet, but not only is that impossible, but I would never attempt to. It was terrible, life-altering, and I'm forever changed, but it was the most important part of the performance. Something I could never have planned and never replicated exactly the same. It was brutal and honest, as art should be.

Reporter: Hmm, I see. Is there anything you'd like to tell our readers about your latest piece?

Fleiss: Before you lash out, look at yourself. Are you accomplishing anything with your anger? Your outrage? Or are you just bringing more pain into the world?

Fleiss went quiet for several years, having lost her custody battle for her daughter and focusing on paintings that she refused to loan out for display, living a private life with her partner Shelia. Then in late 2020, as the pandemic overtook the world and she struggled with her mental health having separated from her partner, she found her voice again and set up her first performance since "Streaming," this one titled "Broken," and dedicated to her Shelia. Please feel free to explore the tactile experience of running your hands through the pebbled glass from the performance while you listen to an of "Broken," performed on the streets of New York City, where the artist constructed a box out of tempered sheets of glass around herself.

Broken, November 30, 2020, digital recording.

Fleiss: Is this what you want?
(drum beat)
Fleiss: Broken. Broken me. Broken you. Broken promises.
(drum beat)
Fleiss: Broken world. We are all dying!

Man 1: Shut up!

Fleiss: I just want to be loved. I don't want to die alone.
(sniffling followed by shriek of pain)

Man 2: Oh god, she's got a knife in there! Someone help!

Man 3: Jesus Christ, she slit her arm straight up to her elbow.

Fleiss: No, don't. It's part of the performance.

Woman 1: I can help. I'm a nurse. You call an ambulance.

Fleiss: No! Broken. It's all broken, irreparably so. I'm sick of loneliness and the harsh words of anonymous voices online, whispers in the void. Well, the void calls to me as it calls to us all.

(Glass pane shatters, then the others fall and shatter loudly, beads of glass bouncing along the street and sidewalk)

Fleiss: Don't you see? I bleed for all of you. Look at me and laugh. Go ahead! Hate me. Mock me if you must. I'll be the sacrificial lamb. Just either someone love me or let me die.

Fleiss denied the performance was a suicide attempt but was hospitalized for several weeks following the abrupt end of the piece when an ambulance arrived and treated her injuries. Fans of her work managed to collect the broken bits of pebbled glass for archival purposes, and we hope you can feel the passion in the performance through this combined auditory and tactile experience.

The penultimate work in this collection of performance pieces is the equally controversial "Bully." Performed at this museum in the very room you stand in, "Bully" was a culmination of Fleiss's experiences with online harassment following her hospitalization and subsequent withdrawal from the art world and society in general. While sequestered, she began chatting regularly with anyone who reached out to her, from those who genuinely wanted to form a friendship or praise her art to those who sought her out specifically to hurt and humiliate her. "Bully" consisted of two parts, the first being the artist writing various insults she'd been called onto her nude body in marker (printouts of screenshots of the insults, with usernames not redacted, plastering the wall behind her. For the second part, she invited viewers to hide their faces with provided masks and anonymously write their own commentary about her on her body. The following is an excerpt of an interview about the piece.

Excerpt from interview regarding *Bully*, March 21, 2021, NPR.

Reporter: Performance artist Juniper Fleiss joins us now, having just finished her latest piece "Bully." For this piece, you allowed us into the very personal harassment you've experienced online. What would you like us to take away from this performance?

Fleiss: That the anonymity of the internet age has evolved us into cruel creatures with little regard for other's feelings. As someone who has opened my heart and soul to the world, revealing my struggles with mental illness, loneliness, and violence and pain, I was disgusted by the plethora of online bullies who specifically sought me out to make my life hell. But, as much as it hurt, for I'm only human, it also intrigued me. Why have we become so cruel? Why are we so quick to judge others but unable to turn the mirror on ourselves? What do these trolls get out of their behavior? This piece focused on those questions and hopefully those who participated and witnessed got some sort of answer from what they observed.

Reporter: Your art often revolves around feminist themes. Would you say those themes are present in this latest work?

Fleiss: Of course. I make myself the object that the world wants me to be. Both men and women are victims of the patriarchy, seeing the feminine as less-than, something to be used and discarded, something that only has value as a beautiful object. I am no longer what society deems beautiful, now middle-aged and warped by time and childbirth. What kind of object does that make me? My nude form does not fit the standards our culture demands of a nude woman, and it causes a rush of confusion and anger in many who view it. That is a very important aspect of "Bully," as reading the comments the masked participants left demonstrates just how reviled an imperfect object like myself is seen.

Reporter: You seem so calm and unaffected by the bullying, and yet you admit to struggling with depression. Does the harassment affect you or have you found a way to transcend their insults for the most part.

Fleiss: No, it hurts. It hurts just as much every time, but that is art. That is womanhood. And that is what I want to bring to light in hope that we can realize our transgressions and grow beyond them.

Fleiss's final work, "Touch Grass," has proven so evocative and controversial, that displaying even the short segment playing on the last screen has resulted in protests and outrage against our museum. However, we consider this work to be of great importance despite its graphic nature and have included it with a warning message that displays for thirty seconds, warning of the disturbing footage, before playing the thirty second clip of the performance, live-streamed on April 28th, 2022.

Warning: the following performance piece is considered highly disturbing, and discretion is advised. To proceed with the description of the video clip, final letter by the author, and chat log that accompanied the performance, click the continue button once. Clicking it three times quickly will skip this disturbing segment for those who wish to proceed to the next artist's collection.

You have chosen to proceed to the detailed description and explanation of Fleiss's final work, "Touch Grass". This is your final warning to skip if this was unintentional.

Juniper Fleiss took her own life with her final performance, titled Touch Grass. The performance

19

was streamed for an audience of twenty to thirty viewers, some who cheered her on, some who tried in vain to stop her, but most who watched on in silence, never typing a word into the chat but their presence recorded in the view count.

Posted to the chat, April 28, 2022, 3:04 pm

TheArtisteYouHate: Dear watchers, hiding behind the shield that is your screens, eyes glassy and feet half-asleep from lack of circulation,
TheArtisteYouHate: I know you. I see you, though you think you can't be seen. Disgusting is the only word for what all of you are, what mankind has devolved to, a species of fat globules wasting their lives picking apart the insecurities of others and tearing down any attempt at actual art, all while not contributing anything of their own. Where has art gone? There used to be intellectual discussion, debate, fervent digging into the meaning of time, love, death, life, pain. Now, there's nothing but plastic smiles and cutting words from profile picture-less trolls with names like Zamboni87819 and StarCrusher69. Yes, I see you lurking in my streams, snickering at me before you launch your toothless insults about my age or body or your misunderstanding of art. I don't do this because of you. Don't you dare flatter yourself.
TheArtisteYouHate: I do it because of what we have all become. You are just examples of the rock bottom humanity has hit. I don't want to live

in a world full of shallow, cowardly idiots any longer. There might be a nothingness, a never-ending void, that awaits me, and still that would be better than this living hell of ignorance and pointless cruelty.
TheArtisteYouHate: I tried to show the world the truth through my work, but you all ignored it. Mocked it. Actively destroyed it and me together. I've had enough. It's time for you to reap what you've sown.

Touch Grass, 2022, clips from recording of livestream

(Fleiss sits in high grass, a wooden fence behind her, later confirmed to be her backyard. Sunbeams halo her head as they filter through a tree and a gentle breeze tousles her hair. She is wearing a plain white smock, barefaced with red puffy eyes as if she's been crying. In her hands she holds a gardening machete, its edge brighter than the rest, as if recently sharpened. She waits for two long minutes, staring expressionless into the camera of her laptop. Her breathing deepens as she falls into a trance-like state. She begins to mumble, incoherent at first.)

Fleiss: *unintelligible*

(She takes the blade and positions it against her stomach. Her eyes lift to the sky, her chest moving as her breath quickens. The mumbling stops. She waits in silence for three seconds.)

Fleiss: This is what you want to see. It's what you've all been hoping for, isn't it? Well, you're welcome. Enjoy.

(She draws the blade swiftly inward and then across her belly. Dropping it into the grass on her left side, she screams as she rips at her clothing, already a large stain of dark red blooming across her midsection. As the soaked clothing tears away, her intestines are seen visibly protruding from the deep gash.)

(Fleiss screaming and panting.)

(Her hands dig into the wound and pull out the intestines, spreading them in the grass before her. She falls forward onto her hands and knees, other dark organs spilling from her belly as she wails. She reaches down once more, whimpering as she rubs the innards into the grass, bits of dirt and outdoor debris visibly clinging to the pink intestinal casing as blood pools under her.)

Fleiss: I love you, Delilah. I'm sorry.

(The artist falls forward onto her face, her hair obscuring everything except the white back of her smock and the ever-growing pool of deep red forming around her body. Her back continues to rise and fall for three minutes.)

(Fleiss wheezes and shudders.)

(Her breathing appears to stop. She does not move again until the stream is ended more than an hour later when authorities arrive at the scene).

Selected excerpts posted to the chat between 3:06 pm and 4:17 pm (usernames redacted)

[redacted]: Is she really gonna do it?

[redacted]: Get on with it, old bitch

[redacted]: Gross!

[redacted]: Borrrrrring

[redacted]: Fake
[redacted]: you can tell those are blood packs
[redacted]: stupid whore is always looking for attention

[redacted]: is she dead? she's not moving
[redacted]: quick, somebody poke her with a stick

[redacted]: good. No more of her bullshit "art"

[redacted]: die bitch

No one informed the authorities until 4:09 pm.

She is survived by her daughter, who has changed her name and asks we respect her privacy; however, she did provide the following quote for this collection of her mother's work, specifically this final piece.

"I think her final piece speaks volumes about our modern society and culture. If I could rename her piece, I'd call it "The Evolution of Mankind" instead, because that's what we've become now. Monsters. It's what she tried to show us all along, but nobody listened, or maybe nobody cared."

This concludes the work of Juniper Fleiss. Please continue along the path to continue your experience with our next artist.

About the Author

Emma E. Murray's work has appeared in anthologies like *What One Wouldn't Do*, *Obsolescence*, and *Ooze: Little Bursts of Body Horror* as well as magazines such as *Cosmic Horror Monthly*, *If There's Anyone Left*, *Pyre*, and *Vastarien*. Her chapbook, *Exquisite Hunger*, is available from Medusa Haus, and her novelette, *When the Devil* (Shortwave), as well as her debut novel, *Crushing Snails* (Apocalypse Party), will be coming out Summer 2024. To read more, you can visit her website EmmaEMurray.com.

Content Warnings

Domestic violence, suicide, self harm, child endangerment, child sexual abuse, harassment, abuse, deteriorating mental state

About the Publisher

Archive of the Odd is a micropress specializing in speculative found fiction, run by Cormack Baldwin. It publishes short fiction in the magazine Archive of the Odd.

www.ingramcontent.com/pod-product-compliance
Lightning Source LLC
Chambersburg PA
CBHW040915010826
48978CB00013BB/1297